KISS A ME

Goes to School

Babette Douglas

Illustrated by
Barry Rockwell

Productions

Kiss A Me™ Productions, Inc. produces toys and booklets for children with an emphasis on love and learning. For more information on how to purchase a Kiss A Me collectible and plush toy or to receive information on additional Kiss A Me products, write or call:

Kiss a me™ Productions

Kiss A Me Productions, Inc.
90 Garfield Ave.
Sayville, NY 11782
888 - KISSAME
888-547-7263

About the Kiss A Me Teacher Creature Series:
This delightfully illustrated series of inspirational books by
Babette Douglas has won praise from parents and educators alike.
Through her wonderful "teacher creatures" she imparts profound lessons of tolerance
and responsible living with heartwarming insights and a humorous touch.

KISS A ME Goes to School

Written by Babette Douglas
Illustrated by Barry Rockwell

ISBN 1-89034-309-9
Printed in China

www.kissame.com

To *Theresa M. Santmann,*
Who inspires the teacher in all of us

Preface

*In our wonderful and ever-changing world,
children are our greatest legacy
and investment in the future.
And yet, in the world we have prepared for
them, love seems to have been mislaid.*

*With this little story, one of a series, one
little creature, Kiss A Me, seems to have
found love again and put it into action.*

*With an unshakable belief in kindness,
hope for a brighter future and a loving
desire to make a difference, Kiss A Me
teaches us all...that everyone can.*

The baby whale's mother
Drew close to his ear
And low whispered sweetly:
"It's time, KISS A ME dear.

"To the schools of the fishes
It's time – you must go,
To learn there the lessons
In life you must know.

"Remember your manners.
Be careful and slow.
Don't frighten the schools
Of the creatures below."

The baby whale dove,
Controlling his speed.
"I'll learn here the lessons
In life I might need."

The first creature he met
As he made his descent
Was Rocky the Tuna,
A giant of a gent.

Remembering his manners,
He called, "Howdy-do!"
But Rocky just shrugged
And asked, "Do I know you?"

He swam past some dogfish
Having a fight.
Someone called out,
"There'll be no biscuits tonight!"

Parrot fish called
As through the water they flew,
"Hi ya, sweetie, nice to see ya,
Gotta be goin' – kiss, kiss, toodle loo!"

KISS A ME, with a chuckle,
Kept diving below.
"Those were the oddest fish creatures
I ever will know!"

Down KISS A ME kept going,
'Til there, within sight,
Was the little fish schoolroom.
Students lined up by height!

The desks were all taken
By schools of young fish.
All waited with patience.
No lessons they'd miss.

The teacher rose slowly
To address the waiting class,
A giant octopus lady
With a magnifying glass.

"Look at life clearly.
Life must be held dear.
To give as well as get
Is the reason we're here.

"We each are important.
Our hearts hold a clue.
Ask deep within you:
What good can I do?

"When you find the answer
Your heart says is true,
You may then leave the class
And your good works pursue."

Now mother waited patiently
'Til back to her side
Came her darling KISS A ME
To tell her with pride:

"I've gone to the schools
Of the fishes below.
They've told me the stories
They want me to know.

"Then they all voted
For me on the spot,
Because I've decided
To swim up on top.

"And since I have love
In my heart flowing free,
They voted me speaker
For all life in the sea.

"For all of the wonders
That they've shown to me,
I'll be the best speaker
Anyone ever did see.

"I'll travel quite far
From the place of my birth
To bring the sea's message
To all those on earth.

"But, mother, for now
I will tell only you!
I love all the creatures.
They are beautiful too!

"There are fishes bright silver
And some are quite blue.
Some are all colors
And some every hue.

"Some fast as lightning
And some that are slow.
I'm really excited
By life down below!

"Some creatures are gooey,
Some hard as stone,
Some swim in company,
Others swim alone.

"And, Mother, they loved me.
They gave me to wear
This great starfish medal
For diving down there.

"But they have decided
I've no need to go back.
I'll instead tell the people
Of the one thing we lack.

a"It's LOVE that's the answer
To all that I see.
It's healthy for all
And it's given out free.

"Since people find breathing
In water quite grim
And can't stay the time
Friendship needs to begin,

"I'll be the link
Between the land and the sea.
I'll carry my message
To all who'll hear me.

"And one day earth's children
Will control earth's debris.
They'll respect all the waters
And creatures like me.

"This spirit of caring
Will flow like the tide
To encourage the mammals
who presently hide.

"And wherever I am,
Wherever I go,
I'll send up my kisses
Whenever I blow.

"When my kisses are seen,
Floating high out at sea,
Their message is LOVE…
From your KISS A ME."

KISS A ME loves you...Pass it on!

THE END

Babette Douglas, a talented poet and artist, has written over 30 children's books in which diverse creatures live together in harmony, friendship and respect. She brings to her delightful stories the insights and caring accumulated in a lifetime of varied experiences.

"I believe strongly in the healing power of love," she says. "I want to empower children to see with their hearts and to love all the creatures of the earth, including themselves." The unique stories told by her "teacher creatures" enable children to learn to recognize their own gifts and to value tolerance, compassion, optimism and perseverance.

Ms. Douglas, who was born and educated in New York City, has lived in Sayville, New York for over forty years.

Additional Kiss A Me™ teacher-creature stories:

**Character toys are available for each book.
For additional information on books, toys,
and other products visit us at:**

www.kissame.com